THE ROAD MORE MORE TRAVELLED

Tales of those seeking refuge

Pebblestone

Printed in the United Kingdom

First Printing, 2016

Cover design by Creative Creative Limited

Editing services by Fiction Feedback

Published in 2016 by Pebblestone

ISBN 978-0-9931472-2-7

ACKNOWLEDGEMENTS

This project has only been possible due to the work put in by the following generous people.

Cover design: Alex Horne of Creative Creative Limited.

Editing: Fiction Feedback, www.fictionfeedback.co.uk

Brian Bilston for letting us use his brilliant poem 'Refugees'.

I also received tremendous help in editing, proofreading and general moral support from 'Boz' B E Andre, Ros Davis and Ed Wilson.

Of course none of this would be possible without the authors who have contributed the stories and I want to thank them for writing moving and thought provoking tales.

David Beckler

CONTENTS

<u>INTRODUCTION</u>

During the summer of 2015 our news outlets reported the almost daily death toll of refugees who drowned while trying to reach Europe. Instead of seeing this as the humanitarian disaster it was and calling on our governments to do more to help, many called for more draconian action against those who made it and stronger measures to prevent these desperate people from setting off from North Africa. Ignoring the reasons forcing these people to flee, they suggested we address the 'pull factors', as if the prospect of living in a hostel and getting meagre benefits was reason to abandon your home, family and friends and attempt this perilous journey.

In attempting to justify their stance, they referred to the refugees in dehumanising terms. Commentators and politicians alike used words such as swarm and horde to describe the refugees and warned we were being invaded and would be swamped. The language used brought to mind the utterances of fascist politicians in the 1930s.

As writers we recognise the power of words and wanted to counter this poisonous narrative. This book is our attempt, in a small way, to refute the claims that refugees are less than human and are a threat to us and our way of life.

Refugees

BRIAN BILSTON

They have no need of our help

So do not tell me

These haggard faces could belong to you or me

Should life have dealt a different hand

We need to see them for who they really are

Chancers and scroungers

Layabouts and loungers

With bombs up their sleeves

Cut-throats and thieves

They are not

Welcome here

We should make them

Go back to where they came from

They cannot

Share our food

Share our homes

Share our countries

Instead let us

Build a wall to keep them out

It is not okay to say

These are people just like us

A place should only belong to those who are born there

Do not be so stupid to think that

The world can be looked at another way

(now read from bottom to top)

This is Britain

BEVERLEY BUTCHER

I'd been in the Goyt Valley for two nights and couldn't get a phone signal. The weekend had started with minor annoyances quickly followed by pieces of golden, unexpected luck – or being a jammy git, as Posh Duncan observed. My car was off the road, needing new brake pads and discs, and I'd left it until late on the Friday to do something about it. The garage agreed to keep it, but that meant I had no wheels – until Duncan offered me a lift. He'd planned to go to a protest in Manchester, a big demonstration against air strikes abroad, or anti-austerity, or one of his many other causes. I looked out at the sheep and said, 'Too right, mate,' every so often, pleased he'd decided instead to spend the weekend in the hills, getting off his face.

When we arrived a few people were already gathered; some I knew well, of old, and others – like the hippy woman with dreadlocks and her already stoned boyfriend – I didn't. When I unpacked my tent and found a massive rip in the top, Hippy Woman reached in to her embroidered rucksack, brought out a repair kit and cheerfully tacked the rip together while I applied my lips and lighter to the business end of a bong.

The goodwill that followed me amused Posh Duncan; each time someone handed me food or a spliff, or a good-looking girl sat next to me, Duncan yelled, 'As if by magic, the shopkeeper appears!'

*

We'd not done this for years: met with tents, food, music and drugs, out on a Pennine hilltop or Peak valley. As a city boy, I liked the contrasting remoteness; I loved to stare in to a black sky and listen to the others talk about quarks and dark matter, aliens and faraway planets, music, sex, and politics, always politics. Duncan once asked me where I stood on the Middle East during one such gathering, and I replied that I was on a knotty hummock with something digging into my arse.

Everyone took this as a metaphor and nodded and grunted assent. Duncan took a bong off me and whispered, 'You jammy fucker,' into my ear. Few bongs – everyone's an expert.

On Sunday morning I'd woken up with half a pizza attached to my face. I'd been on a sortie with Duncan to find processed food in the village, because the curry Hippy Woman made looked like wallpaper paste, and she'd put goat in it. We found a little takeaway in a row of terraces.

'As if by magic, Mario's Pizza appears!' exclaimed Duncan.

I was wearing a pair of Aviator sunglasses that didn't belong to me. Last night we'd heard distant rumblings and then seen several very bright and unsynchronised flashes – usually you can count the time between the lightning and the thunder, for example: FLASH! *One … two … three … four …* BOOM!

That's the distance, in miles, of the storm from where you are; it is perhaps coming in fast from America, over Howth Head, moving over Liverpool before dumping its payload on the doorstep of the Pennines. But no storm arrived.

Posh Duncan dropped me off at home at half past six. I groaned a goodbye and decided I'd go straight to bed, falling face down on top of the duvet without undressing or brushing my teeth.

I awoke, cold and with a jangling nervous system from smoking and dehydration, and listened to more distant growling storm sounds. I put the portable telly on, but it was crackling with interference that I assumed was a signal interrupted by atmospheric disturbance. These mad storms.

When seven thirty came, I showered, ate a bowl of cereal standing up, and left the house. I thought a walk to work along the canal towpath would do me good, get rid of the weekend's excesses and all that. Quiet streets slept in half-term silence. I pulled my mobile out and flipped the case open – no signal. Still? Fucking phone company. Couldn't even ring the bastards to complain.

On the foot-worn mud track by the river, I heard Baz on his scrambler bike. I knew him from school, but we'd drifted apart in Year 9, not long after Baz fixed up a single fairground waltzer carriage, attached to part of the spin board, and got it going in the back alley at McGinley Street. Baz had a talent for electronics and mechanics – probably bionics, given the chance. His dad had a garage where he fixed cars and Baz helped, a miniature of his old man in navy overalls, wiping his hands on an oily rag. Knowledge seeped into Baz like damp seeped up the walls in his gran's back bedroom where he kept his electrical equipment.

Baz persuaded me to get in that waltzer carriage, along with Steve, his puffball of a ginger tomcat.

'You'll just have to trust me, Ken,' he said, assuring me of its safety. He nicknamed me Ken because my last name is Barlow and he thought I was a bigger pussy than Steve. His recurrent cries of 'Get on, Ken!' and 'It's sweet, mate!' urged me forwards.

I still have the scars where Steve sank his claws into my face and used it as an anchor until the carriage stopped spinning. After that, there were no more summers of trying to reproduce the hoverboard from *Back to the Future,* or rigging up rudimentary zip wires that would allow us to float outside Mrs Pearson's upstairs windows while she was putting laundry away. We moved from the McGinley Street terraces into a little semi on the other side of town, and left Baz behind.

I was walking along the canal, which had a proper towpath and was pin-straight, into town; Baz was a distance away on the riverbank. I recognised his way of gunning the accelerator.

The riverbank was ancient and meandering, and turned its banked backbone on the canal as if to say *I'm going out to sea. You're just off into town, you whiny little bitch.* There was a point where they met in uneasy confluence, at the old stone bridge that carried traffic into the city. That's when I saw him. Whip-thin, leather-look windcheater, no helmet, his hair the black hedgerow it had been since primary school. My face a waxing moon, my head shaven to disguise baldness, my suit slightly too tight. I adjusted my manbag to sit at the back of my thickening frame. In case Baz saw it. Then I'd be Deirdre, not Ken.

Usual grey-skied morning, the kind Australians moan about when they visit. My job is to walk tourists around the city centre talking about points of historic interest, followed by tea and scones at the art gallery . I like the past. It doesn't make sudden moves or deviate from its path, or one day tell you it's a transvestite. I don't have anything against trannies. I just like safety.

He'd seen me. He was waving his arms and shouting, but I'd put my earphones in when I'd heard his bike so it was like watching telly with the sound turned down. I pulled the earphones out and heard, 'KEN! GET AWAY!'

A giant, juddering wasp-swarm noise seethed towards me from behind and I was knocked off my feet by a large explosion, tumbling down, down, and over, landing on my backside in the river, a fat toddler sitting splat in a puddle. The water was two feet deep and waving with weeds, a mermaid's green hair. Flowing west, I thought, to the Irish Sea. I must have been a bit shocked. I was thinking silly things, looking at little details, like the damp ladybird beetling up the back of my hand. Next thing, Baz's arms had hooked under mine from behind and he was pulling me over to the bank.

'Come on, Ken, mate!' he said. 'Make an effort.'

I righted myself and clambered up behind him. More explosions and rumbling on all sides of us now, mostly to the north, the direction of the city, and less so to the south, the area of the suburb where we'd grown up.

'What the fuck's going on?' I asked. 'Has there been an accident? Has the chemical plant blown up? Is it fireworks?'

A momentary lull in the explosions. The earth stilled. We were sort of OK because of the old stone bridge and the riverbank protecting us like a Great War trench, but an immense shaking and thrumming came from the sky and dropped a lot of small things that sprung in to little flames and danced a little hobgoblin dance before forming a deadly, fiery ring-o'-roses chain. I said a flat 'Oh,' to myself when I looked up and noticed the symbol painted on the hovering aircraft: an RAF roundel.

'The bike!' yelled Baz. 'Get to the bike!'

I threw myself up the bank towards the sound of the scrambler and my backside had hardly touched the seat before we were off, bumping along the bank, curving away from the conurbation.

'As if by magic, the shopkeeper appears,' I said, weakly.

Now I became aware of everything vibrating on its own private frequency – the earth, the bike, the sky, the horizon. My whole body was locked in a rattling tremor I thought would bust me into little pieces.

Landmarks had perished. Half the tower on the tall hotel had disintegrated, and the sycamore trees in the park at the end of its grounds were either burning or wrenched from the earth with their roots showing. At the edge of Greenlees Park was a low perimeter wall where the statue of Lady Adeline Greenlees, who had bequeathed the public space to the town, lay toppled and fractured. A fifteen-foot bomb crater splattered mud obscenely up the trunks of the still-standing sycamores that would have been planted as saplings around the time men my age were being killed in

19

northern France. A little hand rested in the soil next to the lip of the crater and I didn't know if was a plastic doll's hand, or a human one. If I got Baz to stop, and touched it, I could find out. But I turned my head and looked north to the ring road running parallel to us. My teeth were chattering.

The whole thing was playing out like a horror movie etched behind my eyelids. Closing and opening them would not erase what I was seeing. Unearthly, unholy, un-English. Things like this didn't happen here, on the Angel Isle; not for hundreds of years.

I began to weep into Baz's back.

The motorway was broken up, like a discarded Scalextric track, gantries swinging loose, cars as squashed as tin cans in domestic recycling.

The horses in the fields at the riding school were nosing the ground in a huddle at the corner furthest away from the rubble that was once their stables. Baz angled the front wheel left and right, right and left, always deft, and picked his way along the bank for several, silent miles until we arrived at a concreted expanse that was once the foundation for the nursery in an abandoned garden centre. Here we made better progress, speeding along the concrete until again reduced to the slow, regular bump of the riverbank. Two, maybe three miles on and we were in tree-dotted farmland. Barry stopped the bike and laid it down behind a bank of blackthorn. My legs were shaking and I didn't trust them to walk, but I put one foot in front of the other like a chubby Bambi and then sat, ungainly, in the bushes next to Baz, who produced a bottle of water and tipped some of it over my head. My bottom half was still damp from my dip in the river.

'You're bleeding, mate,' he explained.

My hand went to my head, expecting a mass of chopped liver and gore, but only a faint pink imprint came away and my skull seemed intact when I pressed.

Baz looked at my head and said, 'Just a scratch.'

'What's going on, Baz?'

He drank from the water bottle and passed it to me. 'It's complicated, mate.' Baz sighed and creased his face as though he was about to explain algebra to a baby while expelling a hard and troublesome shit. 'You not seen the protests, mate? The riots?'

I trembled and wept and could only say, 'No. No.'

'Fuck's sake, Ken. History's now, mate. This is fucking happening. We're at war. We're under attack.'

'We don't have wars. This is Britain.'

Barry sighed. 'We bombed the Middle East. People no likey. Refugees by the thousands. People no likey. Refugees getting shot at. People no likey. More and more cuts over here, more and more violence abroad, more and more protests, and then it all joined up, mate, and this weekend, in all the cities, the protests kicked off in to riots and the army got involved. Have you not wondered why your phone's not working, why your telly's not showing anything? The revolution will not be televised, mate.'

Another succession of bangs shook the ground like a hideous, rogue Bonfire Night celebration.

'But the RAF are here now!' I said. 'It'll be OK.'

'They're not here to protect us, Ken. They're bombing us, mate. *They're* the ones doing this.'

He stuck out a hand. I felt his palm warm and dry on mine, and he pulled me to standing.

'I've got a plan, mate. You'll just have to trust me,' he said.

I thought of the countless drains I'd got stuck in, the times I'd got entangled in brambles like a fly caught in a spider's web, had the front of my hair singed off, been hurled from the back of something moving immensely fast, spent hours in fracture clinics; Baz had always been there, getting me in to it … and getting me out of it.

He picked up the scrambler, kicked it in to action, and we were away; Baz and I, years dissolved, heading west.

Long

BRETT N WILSON

A feather, the ancient Egyptians said, could serve as a weight on scales used for the weighing of souls. Alexander, thinking he saw one, reached down quickly before it was trampled, and placed it in a pocket. Then he ran a finger over one of its rilled edges to make sure it was real.

The snow was at least two feet thick. If you were at the front of the line, it meant either walking in the usual manner, so that you had to push the weight of snow forwards, or you could lift your legs and thrust down. Either way made your thighs and hips ache. The guards changed the lead periodically, so the front man could rest, but if they put you near the back you were slipping in mud in a white walled levy. Careering sideways, the insubstantial snow parted as you fell.

The tops of barley stubble in the quilted fields looked exhausted. Black lines petered into the distance, where there was an occasional flurry of smoke. They were like a centipede, trudging through the snow, leaving a distinctive signature, visible until redacted by the weather.

He saw Gregory look back. Alexander observed deep sunken eyes, the cheekbones of starvation. The hands were thin, almost feminine. Gregory always walked in front. He was older by at least ten years. Alexander knew many things about him, gleaned from watching him move. His legs were failing. He had seen men weaken many times. The lower body confirmed it. Instead of the normal gait, they elaborated. They made elliptic strides. The hips would be looser, the shoulders erratic.

When he first sat next to Gregory, the old man would whisper about his family over his steaming potatoes, the greying whiteness of his whiskers opalescent and ghostly. In truth, there was little to say except complain. But there were lots of stories in the eyes. Like the body, the face was a book.

His own family seemed like wraiths now. Gregory had told him that the real purpose of the march was to take away memory.

'But they want to kill us, Grigor. They want to drive us into the snow.'

'No Sasha,' Gregory said. 'They want to make us forget.'

The horizon looked like a grey pencil stroke etched on white, periodically interrupted by a mound of rocks. This was north of the arctic line, where vegetation found it hard to survive. To Alexander the stunted limbs of a tree looked like a man in pain. There was blue light caressing the gullies, playing on a valley in the distance. A mountain seemed to shimmer.

Then he felt himself slipping and falling sideways but he could do nothing. The man in front kept going. As he struggled to right himself, Alexander noticed dirt between his fingers, cold and powdery, not at all how dirt should feel. As he squeezed, it warmed in his hands, but he knew his hands weren't really warm at all. He was inches from the edge of the road and a guard was punching him. The guards were unpredictable. Sometimes they beat a man to death because he couldn't walk any more. They used the butts of their rifles, the moans filling your ears, until among the grey of coats, there would be a sudden splash of red. He held out an arm and the guard stopped. It took a few seconds to get to his feet, while the world was still rocking. The line had kept moving and he wanted to get back to Gregory so he pushed hard with his legs.

One of his fingers was bleeding, but it would freeze in a second. He put the hand in a pocket, which was filled with potato peelings. He pushed several pieces into his mouth as he caught up with Gregory. Alexander ate even rotting, spoiled food. He ate carrot tops and onion peel, and like an animal he chewed grass to keep infection and fever away. Alexander would eat the vomit of another man, to stay alive.

He wanted to sleep and dream of warmth. It wasn't a warm bed he imagined, it was warmth itself. He dreamt of phlogiston, a fluid heat which could saturate his bones. If cold had the power do that, why not heat? He would dream of it until he felt warm or until he could dream no more.

But he knew he must keep going. He knew the routines. They always walked a couple of hours before breakfast, before the first pure drops of sunlight lit the pencil line of grey. Then they sat down in circles of a dozen and arranged the pots. Sometimes it was lentils and sometimes it was cabbage. Sometimes it was lentils and cabbage. Every now and again it was potatoes or onions. Occasionally, if the guards were impatient, they would pour a little petrol over the kindling and they would apportion the vegetables and any meat to the pot. The favourite addition was sausage, mostly made of fat. It sounds perverse, but fat is comforting. It's something you crave. Think about it while you are walking and your tongue will be awash with saliva. But there was never any sausage in the morning. Mouths were mostly dry and voices hoarse. After breakfast Alexander had rested his head for a second before they had him up and marching.

*

It had become colder over the last few days, cold enough to freeze the moisture on the surface of an eyeball. You mumbled through a scarf which was stuck to the face, if you mumbled at all. Mostly, the only

28

thing you could see was a grey coat in front. Your legs ached. Other constants: feet in searing pain and ankles caked in sores.

The wind was blowing again, driving snow into faces. The journey that has no destination, that just goes on, is not a journey at all. That is what Gregory would say. These men trudging in the snow, many would drop with exhaustion, frostbite, but there would always be men in front and always others behind. Forever a line, marching. Sometimes, when the light was fading he seemed to see them in his mind's eye, leaning forward like spikes driven into snow. Or they might be made of paper, like cut-out dolls, black against white, two dimensional, no longer alive.

'When we view where we've come from we only see a blank and when we look ahead we see the same,' Gregory told him. 'They want to take the memory of our lives.'

It was difficult to see. There was something brooding ahead that might be a storm, or a blizzard, because there was no longer a landscape. It was as if a white wall had shrouded the eyes. The guards called out and began arranging the walkers in tight circles. That meant that they must crouch down. It would be no use lighting a fire under the dark hue of the sky. They would face inward, where one of them would be given an ember in a pair of tongs. The ember glowed at first, providing a meagre radiance. Each circle would be covered with a blanket before the guards brought a pot which was usually full with vegetables, but was now filled with hot stones. The blanket reached over their backs and down so that they could sit on the edge, stopping a gust from whipping it away. They joined and waited it out. Some men would die. You hoped it wouldn't be you.

The next day was another aching walk with no respite. Gregory was in bad shape.

'Do you know the date, Sasha? Have you been counting the days, like I said?'

'Yes Grigor, I won't forget.'

Gregory had not eaten. Tears were falling on his cheeks, leaving a frozen trail, getting thinner and slowing as each became turbid. Gregory smiled. There were four teeth left. He lifted his hands as if to bless

Alexander, blue veins on pallid hands, a smile with the infinite love of humanity and myriad pains lodged in every wrinkle. If not the desire to create, the passion to live; if there was only emptiness inside us, there would be no escape. Alexander could see that.

That evening, lying on his back, the sky had become a huge disc and to one side he could see a mountain reaching upward. He felt as if he was about to be loosed from his body, to float among where the stars shone most brightly. He wanted to reach out to them. They were the other, the something outside his life from which he felt separated by his cold, his aching, but still he imagined that in that infinite sky there were angels careering and swooping.

The next day Gregory died. The guards left him by the side of the road. At first Alexander could see the still form, but each time he turned the figure was smaller and whiter under the falling snow. Alexander pulled the feather from his pocket. It was the weight of Gregory's soul. And as he let the wind take it, he imagined it turning higher and higher in the air until finally it was with the angels.

From the collection of short stories "Stalin's Breakfast"

The One That Got Away

DAVID BECKLER

The shoal of Bluefin swam north and the small fishing boat followed. Even an undersized fish would make this a good month. Karim stood in the bow, anticipation heightening his senses. The boat swooped into the trough of a wave and climbed up the other side. A faint smell reached him. The odour increased, filling him with unease, until it made him gag. This must have been the same stench given off by the slave ships when they'd crossed the Atlantic. The source was still over the horizon and he had no wish to go closer. He signalled to Ridwan, and, with a look of frustration, his son pulled on the tiller until the stink lay behind them.

A sense of loss infused Karim as they continued fishing, and each puny specimen they caught seemed to mock his decision. The sun dipped towards the horizon and he told Ridwan to return home. Their meagre catch half-filled one basket. Disappointment, a constant companion nowadays, made Karim's limbs heavy. They arrived at the harbour in darkness. Instead of the bustling port of a few years ago, now just two small craft like theirs swayed in their moorings. When he'd given this old boat to his former captain, Karim hadn't expected to put out to sea in it again.

The fishmonger waited on the quayside. Although ancient and bent, he exuded an air of menace. Karim and his son carried the basket between them and placed it on the old man's scales. Claw-like hands pecked at the contents as he examined the miserable catch. He sucked his gums before spitting out a figure, even less than Karim had feared. Not having the energy to haggle, he ignored his son's look of disbelief and accepted the money.

They walked home in silence. 'They were worth more,' Ridwan said finally.

Karim ignored him.

'We should have chased the tuna,' his son persisted.

34

Karim pondered the best way to tell Eisha what had happened.

'Those dirty animals are ruining everything.'

Anger made his chest tighten. *Haven't I taught you better?* But his son was right, *and* wrong. It wasn't the refugees who were causing the problems. Karim's mind drifted back to Beirut in '82, from where he had escaped with his parents but without Anisah... tears burned at the corners of his eyes. He still couldn't think of his little sister without pain.

The gates of their compound gaped. He wished the bloody tailor wouldn't keep leaving them open. A group of loud men sat on the veranda, *his* veranda, smoking and drinking tea.

The tailor shouted an overfamiliar greeting. 'Welcome home, Karim. "Home is the sailor, home from the sea." Have you brought the fruits of the deep with you?' His cronies giggled at the witticism.

Karim swallowed his irritation and smiled. 'Good evening, gentlemen.'

At least the tailor paid rent; the money supplemented the meagre sums Karim made now from fishing. Eisha was in the kitchen where once she'd ruled, commanding a cook and a maid, and which she now shared with the tailor's wife.

'Welcome back, Mr Malouf,' the tailor's wife said. 'God be praised for bringing you home safe.'

'Thank you.' He bowed to the good woman.

His wife's gaze interrogated him before flicking to Ridwan and seeing the answer on his face. She sighed and turned back to the cooker. Karim ignored his wife's insult and trudged to the small shower room to wash. Once a private space reserved for him and his wife, they now shared it with their sons, leaving the larger bathroom for their paying guests.

During the meal, he studied Ilias. He was fifteen and almost old enough to join them at sea. But his club foot made him clumsy; a liability in a small boat. Unlike Tareq, he didn't have the brains to go to college; not that Karim could afford to pay for another son to be educated.

'Tareq needs to buy another textbook,' Eisha said, breaking into his reverie.

'How much?'

She told him. More than he'd made today.

'We saw Bluefin,' Ridwan said. 'We had to stop—'

'The law says we can't catch them,' Karim interrupted.

'—because of a refugee boat.'

Eisha made a sound of disgust. 'Those dirty cockroaches will ruin our country. Like a filthy tide pushing us into the sea.'

'You can't blame them—'

'If it wasn't for them, you would still have the *Sea Wind*.' Her voice rose, making sure the men on the veranda heard. 'We wouldn't be sharing our beautiful home with these ignorant people.'

'The refugees didn't take my boat.' *Friends of your cousin did*.

She waved his denial away. 'They are the cause.'

Karim couldn't summon the will to argue with his wife.

*

The fisherman and his son left home before dawn and reached the harbour while it was still dark. Karim checked the fuel, just enough to get to the nearest fishing ground. They hugged the coast and the morning's catch was better than expected. They filled three baskets and an unfamiliar optimism infused Karim. Around four, they headed back, throttle down to conserve fuel. Tomorrow, they'd have a full tank.

As they approached the harbour two specks appeared in the sky, travelling low and fast. Ridwan's young eyes identified them first.

'French Air Force.'

Karim's memory of similar planes destroying Gaddafi's forces awoke mixed feelings. The two aircraft separated, one dropping back and the other levelling off. Then it seemed to jerk before peeling away, leaving two smaller objects following its earlier trajectory.

'Rockets, Dad!' Ridwan shouted.

Karim stared in disbelief for a moment as the specks grew. Then he roused himself and opened the throttle. He pushed the tiller hard and the boat swung about. The baskets shot across the deck and one flew over the gunwale. A second followed. With a cry of despair Ridwan dived for it, hooking the handle before it disappeared. The thud of a detonation filled Karim's ears and a column of water drenched him. A second explosion, further away, created a silent waterspout and his ears rang. Ridwan dropped the now half-empty basket, scrambled to his feet, and, uttering a soundless roar of rage, waved his fist at the receding aircraft.

The second jet peeled away, its missile pods still attached. Karim's heart fluttered and his ears felt hollow. Ridwan said something Karim couldn't hear and knelt at the edge of the boat, reaching into the water. Dead fish floated around them but whether from the explosion or his lost basket Karim couldn't tell.

After checking the skies, he aimed the boat towards the harbour. The engine spluttered, but his gentle coaxing kept it going until they nosed into the stone quayside. Half their catch had gone, as well as a basket. A heavy weight settled in his gut. As the

39

fishmonger weighed the fish, treble yesterday's despite the losses, Ridwan pointed behind him. A column of dense smoke rose above the horizon from the direction in which the planes had disappeared.

Karim watched it grow until the fishmonger's nasal tone interrupted him. 'These are very small fish, bony—'

'Don't try to cheat me, old man.'

The fishmonger fixed him with a cold stare. 'These two are damaged and—'

Karim snatched the offending fish from the top of the basket and threw them into the water. A flock of screaming gulls swooped and ripped the flesh apart. He stood, arms folded. With a sigh, the fishmonger upped his offer.

They left the harbour with five times the money they'd taken last night, but thoughts of the lost basket robbed Karim of any satisfaction. 'Tell your mother I'll be late,' he said and set off for the teahouse.

The subdued atmosphere at the once lively meeting place almost made him reconsider, until he spotted a few of his cronies sharing a *shisha* on the terrace.

'Karim, you been let off the leash?' Hassan teased.

'Just because I love my family doesn't mean I'm under their thumb.' The unintended sharpness of the retort silenced his friends.

They made space and an extra cup appeared. Karim filled it from the pot of green tea in the middle of the table. The conversation resumed. The talk was of the French warplanes.

'We were just saying they hit a trawler, destroyed—'

The speaker stopped as Hassan glared at him. The news made Karim's stomach drop.

'It wasn't the *Sea Wind*,' Hassan said but his gaze slid away.

The knowledge it wasn't his stolen boat lifted Karim's spirits. 'They fired at me by the harbour.'

A flurry of excited comments greeted this revelation. 'You can claim compensation from NATO,'

41

one of the others said, to universal derision. 'It's true,' he insisted.

The conversation turned to the subject that dominated their lives: how much safer life was under the Great Dictator.

'Don't forget my cousin in Tripoli. He had a beautiful daughter and one of the bastard's sons kidnapped her. Ruined her.'

'At least they gave her a house. This lot would have cut her throat.'

Nods of agreement greeted this observation. More tea arrived and into a lull in the conversation, Hassan said, 'I'm taking a cargo across tomorrow.'

The friends fell silent. Unlike Karim, Hassan hadn't been able to acquire a smaller boat when the bandits took his trawler. This decision to take a refugee boat across was evidence of his desperation. The smugglers paid the captains well, but few returned. If they made it across, the lucky ones were mistaken for more pitiful refugees, provided their passengers didn't denounce them.

'I'm sorry, brother,' Karim said. 'Where are you sailing from?'

Hassan told them and a plan formed in Karim's mind. He returned home and told his wife that he and his son would go to sea for three or four days so they could catch a Bluefin.

*

The next morning Karim and Ridwan left even earlier than usual, laden with provisions. Karim used the money from yesterday's catch to fill the tank and buy an extra drum of fuel. They set off along the coast.

'Why are we going this way? Shouldn't we head north?' Ridwan said.

There was a time when his son wouldn't have dared question him. 'I need to visit someone.'

They neared Karim's destination and the stench hit them, mixed with the faint smell of smoke. A dark hulk lay in the shallows, fumes still rising from its burnt-out superstructure. Hassan was right; it wasn't the *Sea Wind*. Karim brought his boat alongside the ruined trawler and edged the bow round it before cutting the engine.

Now they'd stopped, the sounds of powerful outboard motors reached them. As the light intensified, he saw them; two inflatables carrying their cargo to a trawler. Each dinghy packed with bodies pressed together, an air of defeat and misery hanging over them like a cloud. Ridwan gasped as he recognised the boat, and Karim realised how Hassan had been so sure the missiles hadn't sunk the *Sea Wind*.

'Are we going to get it back?' Ridwan said.

Karim looked towards the shore. At least ten armed men herded their wretched charges while six more manned the two dinghies ferrying them aboard the *Sea Wind*. Already, people filled her decks, packed together like bundles of reeds, and he imagined his pristine holds crammed with unwashed bodies. But still the loading continued. By the time they finished, the hull wallowed in the water and the top of the gunwale was less than a metre above the waves.

A puff of black smoke shot out of the exhausts, followed by the rough growl of the diesel engines, the sound telling him they needed attention. The dinghies lurked between the *Sea Wind* and the land, making sure nobody tried to swim ashore. Karim thought he saw Hassan in the wheelhouse, but among the multitude swarming around it he wasn't sure.

The men in the dinghies waited until the boat reached the horizon and then returned to shore before dragging their inflatables out of the water. Karim started the motor and followed the trawler.

'What will we do?' Ridwan asked.

'We'll follow.' He didn't know what they could do, but Hassan was a good friend and he would have to think of something before they reached land.

'Are we going to tell the Italians those bandits stole our boat? They might let us take it back.'

'Maybe.'

Karim didn't want to crush his son's optimism. Even if they got the boat back, those pirates would just take it off them again. Anyway, he doubted if any of his nets or gear had survived and he didn't have the money to replace them. They stayed below the horizon, following

45

the trawler by the stench of its unwashed cargo. The afternoon wore on and the sea grew rough. Karim worried about the waves breaking over the sides of the *Sea Wind*.

When a distress flare appeared, he didn't hesitate. He opened the throttle. As the underpowered motor pushed them through the water, he imagined the *Sea Wind* sinking, dragging Hassan and all those people under the waves. The mast appeared and relief made him tremble. The wheelhouse came into sight and he could hear the screams of the passengers. At first, they sounded like distant gulls and then they separated into voices as he got closer. The overladen trawler lurched in the swell, every third wave breaking over her. The cries changed into hoarse shouts and the passengers turned towards him. An odd word escaped from the cacophony, imploring him to help, and arms gestured for him to come closer. Two hundred metres from the trawler, he stopped. Another flare went up and then he saw Hassan.

'Hassan, over here!' he shouted.

His friend shouldered his way through the teeming mass towards the edge, but hands grabbed him.

'Please let my friend go!' Karim shouted.

A gabble of voices replied and he made out a few words in Arabic. 'For the love of God, help us!'

How many could he take? Maybe twenty, but there were hundreds. A large wave hit the trawler, making it shudder, and the cries for help grew more urgent.

'Over there!' Ridwan cried, gesticulating into the distance.

A speck grew larger. It was too slow to be a jet. Then the thrumming of the rotors carried over the sea. One by one, the people on the boat copied Ridwan's urgent gesture and new cries of hope arose. Hassan broke free and dived over the side. He thrashed through the water and Karim surged closer as the sound of the helicopter increased. Hassan was less than a hundred metres away. Something fell from the trawler, a body diving into the sea. The man soon overhauled Hassan. More followed and the water between the two boats boiled.

Hassan struggled, the waves and his clothes dragging him back. The first man reached them while Hassan was still ten metres away. The man grabbed the side amidships and hauled himself up, pulling the boat over before slipping back into the water.

'At the bow!' Ridwan shouted, but the man didn't understand and tried again.

A wave broke, swamping the boat. Without thinking, Karim picked up an oar and slammed it on to the man's skull. The man screamed before disappearing under the waves. Hassan reached them and gripped the gunwale by the bow, gathering his strength to clamber aboard. Ridwan ran to him and grabbed his top before hauling him into the boat. Other hands seized the sides of the boat, threatening to overturn it.

Karim thrust the oar at the nearest swimmer, but he needed a second blow to make the man let go. Sickened by what he'd done, Karim paused. But then the fear of losing his boat galvanised him. Too ashamed to look at them, he used the oar to shove the remaining swimmers away. A young woman held a bundle and, as he jabbed at her, she threw it into the boat before disappearing under the sea. The helicopter was hovering over the trawler, its downdraught flattening the waves and the roar of its engines masking other sounds. The trawler shuddered before a towering wave, triggering shrieks of terror. More people dived into the water and swam towards Karim's little boat.

Hassan lay in the keel, gasping like a fish. Karim opened the throttle. More hands grabbed on to the side but the current snatched them away, leaving people bobbing in his wake. The deck of the trawler now stood level with the waves and dark heads dotted the sea.

Karim stopped. He couldn't just abandon them.

'Are we going to help them?' Ridwan said.

If any of them got too close, Karim, Ridwan and Hassan would be overwhelmed. Even if they picked a few off the edge, it would give others time to reach them. Just a couple of them panicking could drag the boat over. Karim took a deep breath and opened the throttle, not looking back. Hassan sat up in the bottom of the boat.

'Thank you, my friend. I was sure my last moment—'

A feeble cry cut through his speech. The bundle moved and Ridwan picked it out of the water sloshing about in the keel.

'It's a baby,' he announced.

Tiny and wrinkled, it could only have been a few days old. Hassan, father of four young children, took it. 'It's hungry. Do you have anything?'

The baby refused the leftover tea from their flask. Too exhausted to cry for long, it soon fell quiet. The three men sat in silence, close together but each isolated in his thoughts. Karim pushed the images of the *Sea Wind* floundering to the edge of his mind, but the face of the young mother wouldn't leave him. He worried about Ridwan, hoping he hadn't seen her. Desperate to get away from the scene, he ran at full speed but the image didn't fade. They arrived back before nightfall. As they berthed, he studied the baby, who stared back, unblinking.

'What are we going to do with it?' Ridwan said.

Hassan wouldn't meet Karim's gaze.

'We'll take it home,' Karim said, to Hassan's clear relief.

Karim tied a sling for it and, collecting the remains of their provisions, accompanied his son home. Eisha's surprise at their early return changed to outrage when she saw what they'd brought with them.

'Why have you brought this monkey—'

'It's a baby.'

'One of the disease-ridden—'

'You cannot turn an orphan away.' The image of the young mother as the oar struck her forehead, never far from Karim's mind, loomed again. Had she smiled, knowing she'd saved her baby? At that moment, Karim knew he'd do anything to keep the infant safe.

'Don't expect me to take care of it.' Eisha flounced out of the room.

The tailor's wife arrived in the kitchen. 'You found a baby?' She took the infant from him. 'It needs changing. I heard a ship went out today – did they leave this one behind?' She tut-tutted. 'Some women shouldn't have children.'

She left and Karim wanted to shout his defence of the baby's mother. He relived the moment, imagining his hands tightening on the smooth timber of the oar as it jerked when he hit her. Then she disappeared. Could he have saved her?

The tailor's wife returned with the baby. 'I've cleaned her up, but you need provisions for her.'

'I'll get everything tomorrow. Can you take care...'

'I'll do what I can tonight, but I can't look after her in the daytime. I have to work with my husband in the shop.'

Karim wondered if his mother-in-law would help. He'd ask her tomorrow. Now, he didn't have the strength. Eisha came back into the kitchen.

'How are you going to pay for food and clothes? You can't even afford your own son's education.'

Karim ignored her rebuke and made a suggestion he hadn't yet dared broach. 'We should get rid of the car.'

'Aiee! How will we travel to visit Tareq? Do you want to abandon him completely?'

'We don't need a Mercedes. We can buy something cheaper.' He'd never wanted the car in the first place, preferring his old Toyota pick-up.

Anger flared briefly in Eisha's eyes before fading and she bowed. 'Whatever you think best, husband.'

She seemed to shrink, and busied herself with preparing food. The spirited woman he'd married had aged in the last few years. His irritation turned to sympathy. No longer having the luxuries she'd got used to must be difficult, as must sharing her house. At least he got away every day, spending time at sea. He thought back to five years ago with nostalgia. However tough life had been under the Great Dictator, Karim had been able to run a business, make money and provide for his family.

*

The next morning, Karim went to the market. On the way, he saw his old captain wearing rags and trying to sell two pathetic fish he must have caught with a line from the shore. Karim remembered the man's expression when he'd told him he needed his old boat back. The woman in front of him began haggling with the fish seller and Karim hurried past, filled with shame. He bought items for the baby, guilt tugging at him as he paid; this was the money for Tareq's medical books.

He hurried home by another route and gave his purchases to Ilias, who'd shown an unexpected aptitude with the baby. With the promise to take the girl to the local midwife and get her umbilical cord removed, his youngest son waved them off.

The fuel tank was full but, with no money left, Karim wasn't sure how long it needed to last. They set off for the fishing ground of two days ago, hoping for similar success. Soon after they arrived, Ridwan shouted a warning. The roar of outboard motors echoed off the sea. Karim's stomach lurched and he turned for home, coaxing every ounce of speed from the vessel. Despite his efforts, the motors closed in on them. Ridwan's expression, as he watched their pursuers, made Karim's heart race and he willed the boat to go faster. Before long, two inflatables appeared alongside them, so close their wash made his boat rock.

54

Armed men lining the craft observed him with eyes like wet flint. Their expressionless faces told him his life meant nothing to them. Bowing to the inevitable, he slowed.

'Over there,' their leader said, pointing towards the beach.

As Karim neared the shore, the wind carried the stench of putrefaction. Then he noticed the brown cloud of vultures. This must be the killing ground, where they left the bodies of their victims. But why did they kill them on land, instead of dumping them for the sharks? When they reached the shallows, the leader told him to cut the engine. Karim's breath shuddered. This must be it. The end. Then he swallowed. If it was God's will, who was he to argue? Two men leapt out of the nearest dinghy. They waded towards them and, grabbing the bowlines, pulled the boat on to the sand.

The men carried no guns and Karim wondered if he and his son would be spared. Then he noticed the curved dagger each wore in their belts. Since those fanatics had started in Iraq, more of these groups used traditional weapons to murder their victims. A sudden urge to survive made him wonder if they could overpower the two men. The others in the dinghies would soon finish them, but at least they'd have fought.

'Get out,' one of the men said.

Should they jump them now? But Ridwan was already on the sand. Karim joined his son and, as they waded ashore, he whispered, 'Let's attack them when they try to make us kneel.'

Before Ridwan could respond, the outboard started and their boat moved out to sea. The two inflatables followed. Karim recognised Eisha's cousin, hiding at the back of the furthest dinghy, and realised why the bandits had spared them. He climbed up the beach and crested the dune. Below him lay a field of corpses, some already skeletons, but others surrounded by swarms of scavengers tearing at their flesh.

The face of the baby's mother flashed through his mind. And then another image, the *Sea Wind*, full of screaming young mothers and babies, sinking to the bottom of the sea. The picture stunned him, taking his breath away. He blinked and shook his head, closing his eyes with his fingers, but nothing would wipe it away.

But maybe, maybe… he looked at Ridawn. His son would help him. Together they could stop it happening to others, then the vision might fade.

End of the season

ROS DAVIS

The end of the season is near and for Nikos this is the last week of the job he loves in the bar in Kos Town. This bar has real character; it has only been open a year but is never empty. He's going to miss it. Kallia is a good boss but now she needs pretty girls to attract custom over the winter. Nikos understands this; it's business, and things are even harder this year. But he's twenty two and he needs to be established in work.

His girlfriend Gia has come to the bar with one of her friends. She's turned up every night this week to support him. That means a lot. Since her father became unemployed and her chance to go to university disappeared the only work she's managed to find is a few hours here and there in shops. She could have dropped him and aimed for someone who's a better prospect but she hasn't, so far. He would like them to get married soon but Gia's parents will never agree unless he can find work. There's no hope of that in the winter, and things may not be any better in the spring.

She gives him a smile that helps him put on a cheerful face for the customers.

*

At 4 am, Kallia's partner, Yannis arrives to help her close up and to walk her home. He is so lucky to have a good job in a bank, with savings and enough money to give Kallia financial support to open the bar. He and his brother, who has a taxi stand at the airport, have done well, but like their cousin, whose family runs a hotel, they depend on tourism.

Kos Town and the other resorts have lost a lot of tourists this year and everyone knows it's because of the way the foreign media have presented the refugee situation. They all know of people who usually come on holiday but who've cancelled or gone somewhere else because they thought Kos would be overrun with refugees who would cause trouble, bring disease, even attack them. All the shops, restaurants and hotels have been badly affected but Kallia has been lucky, the bar has done better than some others have.

Quite a lot of the tourists who come to the bar ask where the refugees are and has there been much trouble. They say how surprised they've been to find everything the same as usual.

'It's only the area where the refugees must wait to be processed,' the bar staff tell them. 'Usually they're only there for a day or two before they're taken to Athens.'

Others have told of going to look at the camp and how they went back to their hotels in tears. 'I felt so sorry for them,' they say.

Now Nikos shakes his head. If the tourists stop coming ... he can't let himself think about it. Instead, seeing Kallia is almost ready to go, he says, 'I could still help with the Friday barbecue.'

'Nikos,' she says, her voice soft. She comes forward and hugs him. 'Thank you. We'll make it a party for you, eh?'

He doesn't know why he offered to help, but he feels warm inside at the thought of still being part of things. After Friday ... that's another thing he can't let himself think about.

He goes home, letting the soft darkness wrap itself around him as he walks. It's quiet, the streets empty. A breeze comes from the sea, he can smell it. How many refugees will land tonight? He feels a chill: how many will drown?

At home, there's no sound from his parents' or his sister Elena's bedrooms but his grandmother is snoring in the room that used to be his, before her pension was cut in half and his parents took her into their home. Now Nikos must creep quietly into the room he shares with his two brothers. They have to be up early in the morning for school.

He falls asleep, wondering if he should put his name down for the draw to get three months' shift work collecting refuse by night. He knows someone who got that and he said it paid good money.

He doesn't wake until late morning. He smells aubergine and pungent herbs and in the kitchen he finds his mother and grandmother stirring pans on the stove.

'Nikos, *kalimera*,' they greet him.

'*Kalimera*,' he answers. 'That smells good.'

'You can help us,' Grandmother says. 'As soon as Gia brings the paper cups.'

'Gia's bringing them?' The day brightens and he eats his breakfast quickly. The smell's made him hungry.

When Gia comes in she's with their friend Kostas who works in a baker's shop. He looks tired.

'Four hundred and fifty last night,' he says. 'Four of those death-trap boats wrecked, but no one drowned.'

'Thank God,' his mother says. She and Grandmother bow their heads and say a prayer.

'You were there this morning as well?' Nikos asks Kostas. 'With Panagiotis and his bread?'

Kostas nods, as he and Gia arrange their loads of paper cups on the plastic-covered table.

Nikos carries a pan from the stove to the table. 'I don't know how Panagiotis keeps going, making all that bread every day as well as everything for the shop,' he says.

'I don't know how *you* keep going, Kostas,' Nikos' mother says. 'Helping with all the things collected for the refugees and working with Panagiotis to take the bread to them in the morning and then you're on the beach in the night. It's too much.'

'We'll rest in the winter, when they stop coming.'

Nikos' mother shakes her head. 'Too much,' she says, as she collects spoons.

With four of them it doesn't take long to spoon the food into the cups and snap on the lids, then load them on to the trays from the delivery van Kostas has brought.

'Can you manage,' Gia asks Kostas, 'if I stay and help clear things up?'

'Of course. We have a lot of volunteers today,' he says, shaking Nikos' hand and exchanging kisses with the women before setting off in the van.

When Nikos finishes getting ready for work his mother has gone to her supermarket job. Gia is waiting for him. 'I could walk up to the bar with you, if you like,' she tells him.

He smiles. 'I like,' he says.

They walk along the front, heading to the street that goes up to the bar, passing the harbour where private boats and all the little fishing boats moor, round to the part where the tourist trip boats are and the row of restaurants across the road. It's a lovely sunny day, a cloudless blue sky with just a little breeze so it isn't too hot. The harbour scene, with the low hills in the distance is so beautiful they stop every now and then just to look at it, something they don't normally have time for.

'I wouldn't want to live anywhere else,' says Gia. 'My father was talking last night about going to America but none of us wants to go.'

Nikos feels as if she's punched him in the stomach.

'He lived there when he was young,' she says. 'He had a great time. That's what he thinks it's like now, but I'm not so sure.'

'I hope you don't go,' he says. 'But if it's the only way to find work...'

'I'd be miserable,' she says, taking his hand.

He puts his arm round her and keeps it there as they walk.

*

Next day the expected storm comes, with rain pouring in torrents for the whole day and into the night. The rain floods the streets; the school playground becomes a lake which gushes out of the gate like a river in spate. Cars drive as slowly as they can but still send up sheets of water all round them.

When Nikos reaches the bar he's drenched. He won't see Gia tonight. Only the bravest tourists are out, wading through water to restaurants where they can sit inside. The bar is busy later on, but takings are down. Many people in the bar talk about the refugees and how awful it must be for them with no proper shelter, how wet and cold they must be.

*

On Thursday morning Nikos wakes to the sound of weeping. He rushes downstairs and finds Elena sobbing in the kitchen, his mother and grandmother staring at her with wide eyes, both holding the stirring spoons they were using.

'They might as well give up,' Elena is saying, her face wet with tears.

'What?' he asks. 'Who? Give up what?'

'The Argos restaurant,' his mother says. 'What's happened, Elena?'

'No one's going there any more, the smell from the refugee camp's so bad. There's so many of them, they've spread out so much the restaurant is almost surrounded now. They'll have to close down.'

'No, oh no,' their mother says. 'They can't.' She pulls Elena into her arms. 'Oh, poor Sakis.'

'Yes,' Elena says, 'tomorrow, he's just told me, they're deciding tomorrow what to do, who to let go. Sakis is the last one they took on.' She buries her head in her mother's shoulder.

Grandmother looks on and her eyes go hard. 'Well, now we'll see what his fool of a mother says. Now we'll see.'

'What do you mean?' Mother stares at her, still holding Elena tight. 'Can't you see what that means for Elena, for her marriage? How can you be so cruel?'

Grandmother stiffens, her mouth tightens. 'I can see more than you, my dear. What it means is Sakis will be dependent on Elena. On Elena's earnings. It puts her in a much stronger position, doesn't it?'

'But she'll give up her job when they get married,' Mother says.

Grandmother makes an impatient sound in her throat. 'Do I have to spell it out? Sakis is a waiter. Elena's job at the hotel is much better. The hotel that stays open in the winter for all those conferences, which depend on the Argos, which is their restaurant, to provide lunch and dinner for the conference guests.'

Mother's eyes start to shine, a smile appearing on her face. 'Of course! You're right!' She lifts Elena's face. 'D'you see, my love? Now, if Sakis loses his job we can insist you need to keep yours, and live here. None of that nonsense about going to live with his mother, buried in that village at her beck and call. Your grandmother is a wise woman, isn't she?'

Nikos smiles as he too gets it. 'They think a lot about you at the hotel,' he says. 'They'll want you to stay. And then you can persuade them to keep Sakis on at the restaurant for the winter.'

'Nikos!' Mother says. 'Of course she can. Your mother-in-law will be in your debt, Elena!'

'Sakis won't like it,' Nikos warns.

'He won't know. None of us will tell him, will we? And his mother won't!'

'But I don't want him to lose his job,' Elena says, with a sob.

'Of course you don't. But we'll make sure it's only temporary,' Mother tells her, stroking Elena's hair.

'I hope you're right,' Nikos says.

*

As he walks to work his mind keeps going over Elena's situation. She worked so hard, studying to get her qualifications, always hoping one day to be at least an assistant hotel manager, but since Sakis proposed all she's thought of is getting married. She found her wedding dress last week. He hasn't seen it of course but apparently it fits as if it was made for her, which, as she's hiring it, is just as well.

Sakis is an OK guy, Nikos likes him, but he hasn't much money. Yet his family think Elena isn't good enough for their son, as if he's something special. Actually, it's the other way round. Elena shouldn't be burying herself away in the countryside, she's too clever for that. But Grandmother — none of them could have expected her to break away from tradition like that. Still, she's never liked Sakis' mother. But good for her!

He's at the bar before he knows it.

All through his shift the Argos keeps returning to his mind, and what will happen if it has to close.

Several people talk about the next day being his last. 'We'll come to the barbecue,' they say, quite a few tourists among them.

'It'll be a good night,' he tells them, but it won't be for him.

*

At closing time he decides to walk home the long way round, to see for himself what's happening at the Argos.

The night is quiet in the moonlight until he nears the narrow strip of beach. He heads towards the town, the sea on his right. Ahead, lights are moving and as he gets nearer there's the sound of activity and voices coming from the beach.

The lights show dark shapes. People. A lot of people. There's a sense of urgency, an edge of fear to the voices. Children wail and cry.

Nikos runs, until he can make out a crowd of people at the sea's edge, many wearing life jackets. Men wade up to their thighs in the water, further out more are waist-deep.

A shaft of moonlight illuminates a long strip of sea, like a pathway, and lights up figures clinging to something Nikos can't make out.

As he gets nearer he can see it's a boat, or what's left of it. A mass of people are fighting their way into the water from the beach, to reach those struggling to hold on to what's left of their boat. At the same time more are pushing themselves out of the sea, carrying children or helping other people, slipping back as they near the edge where the beach shelves and low waves pull them back.

Most are wearing life jackets, but all the children have are little armbands, as if they were playing in a swimming pool.

Nikos wades in to help.

It's some sort of rubber dinghy and most of its air is gone. People are frantic and panicking, snatching at children and possessions and crying out.

The water is up to his hips and he's drenched by people's frantic splashing but he pushes himself on, doing whatever it takes to get people to the beach.

At last a shaky dawn illuminates exhausted people lying in heaps, clinging to each other. As they revive, some stagger to other heaps where rescuers have piled lumpy bundles, bags, rucksacks, suitcases. Women hold babies and tiny children, all of them wet through; men rock older children, families hold each other, many praying. Some laugh, some are kissing the ground and calling out in English about freedom.

Rescuers gradually form themselves into groupings. Those who seem to know what they're doing move to help reunite people with whatever has been salvaged. Uniformed guards, soldiers, police and volunteers in bright yellow jackets start to organise people and move them to the temporary refuge of the camp. Passers-by, like Nikos, stand or sit around, not sure what to do next.

Nikos starts to shake. A video of what nearly happened is playing in his head.

'Nikos, man, what are you doing here?'

Nikos turns a weary head to the voice. It's Kostas.

'Come on, man, you're soaked. I've got towels in the van, let's get you a bit drier and I'll take you home.'

'I nearly lost a child,' Nikos says, his voice raw and choked. 'Her hand just slipped out of mine. I nearly lost her, a little girl. My God, Kostas. I grabbed for her and all I got was one of those stupid armbands.'

'But you didn't lose her?'

'No. She fought me, she was lashing out with her arms, I went under but I got hold of her legs. She held on to me then. Holy Mother.' He tries to cross himself but he's shaking too much.

Kostas pulls him up, hugs him hard, rubs his back. 'You're shaking man, come with me.'

*

When Kostas drops him off every light in the apartment is on. All the family are there, pulling him in, demanding to know what has happened.

'Kostas brought me,' he says. 'He had to go straight back.'

He can't say another word.

They rush around, get him into a hot shower, tell him to run it for a long time. When he is dry and warm everyone fusses over him, bringing hot coffee, wrapping blankets round him, helping him into bed.

He sleeps till the afternoon, to be woken by his grandmother with fresh coffee.

'I'm making an omelette,' she says. 'You're going to be late, but it's your last day, so what.'

'No, I can't be late.' He leaps out of bed, or tries to, but staggers. He makes it to the bathroom, throws water on his face and head so he feels less groggy. The coffee helps, and so does the omelette he can't resist. Another coffee and he's able to make himself look presentable, wondering at the bruises he finds on his body and remembering he never saw the Argos last night.

Grandmother hugs and kisses him on his way out.

He's half an hour late but no one says anything. Kallia shows him the bar's Facebook page. 'Look at all the comments,' she says.

There are so many comments wishing him well, from locals and pretty much every tourist who has come to the bar over the season. Most of them say they hope he'll be there when they come next year.

The words blur, he rubs his eyes and fusses with some glasses under the bar.

People come in, all of them come straight to him, shake his hand and wish him well, hope he will have a good winter, ask him what he's going to do.

'I don't know,' he says. But he does. He's going to work with Kostas to help the refugees. He's used to working nights, and he'll learn how to be an effective rescuer. And he has to support Sakis, knowing what his mother and grandmother are going to achieve. He lets himself smile. Elena's future mother-in-law has no chance.

As he leaves the bar, unsteady on his feet from all the drinks given to him, Kallia says, 'Next year, Nikos, I want there to be a place for you here.'

No room to dance

ROSIE CULLEN

The girl couldn't even speak English.

Only, 'my nam iz Zofia Stein, pleez to meet.'

Sofia shmia! Jenny thought.

All the neighbours found a reason to be in their front gardens, pruning roses or sweeping their paths, as they watched the thin pale girl arrive with her little brown suitcase.

'How lovely it is for you to have a sister.' Mrs. Corwin from next door patted Jenny's head.

Sister shmister! Jenny thought. She didn't need a sister, her little brother Norman was quite annoying enough already. And at least she didn't have to share her bedroom with him. Her bedroom. With her doll's house and her picture books and her china tea party set decorated with forget-me-nots. Only now there was no room to play. No room to do anything because of the camp bed for Sofia, that Mama said was temporary until they bought a new proper bed.

'Does that mean Sofia is staying forever?' Jenny had asked.

'We'll see,' Mama had replied with a note of uncertainty.

What sort of answer was that? Jenny wondered.

Mama was all fuss, fuss, fuss and then tut, tut, tut and shaking her head all sad when she looked at Sofia. 'Poor child, poor child.'

Ninny more like, Jenny thought. The way she cried at night like a baby. Jenny would give her something to cry about. Yes, that's what she would do!

Worst of all was Papa.

Before Sofia came and spoiled everything Papa would get home from his office and as he came through the front door he would call out, 'who has been as good as gold?' Jenny would rush into his arms and shout, 'I

78

have been as good as gold!' It was a joke, because that was their surname, Gold.

Now when Papa came home all he wanted to do was to talk to Sofia shmia in her funny lingo and they would even sing together as he played his violin. And then when it should finally be her turn for Papa to ask about school and help with her sums Jenny would be shushed because the news would be on the wireless. Papa and Mama would huddle around listening to the wireless all the time now when they were not making a fuss, fuss, fuss over Sofia.

To cap it all Jenny was expected to let Sofia play with all her toys and Mama slapped her if she didn't. It wasn't fair because Sofia had only brought one thing. A music box. A pretty wooden box, intricately carved, and the inside lined with pink satin. But when Jenny picked it up and started to wind the key Sofia had snatched it from her as though Jenny might break it.

And there was an idea. Jenny *would* break it. That would give Sofia something to really snivel about.

Next morning, when Sofia was in the bathroom, Jenny picked up the box and was about to throw it at the wall but then realised she would be in trouble, she would be blamed and Papa might be very angry with her. Gently she replaced the box. She would have to think.

The solution came charging through the door, clambered on to her bed and began to jump up and down. In an instant Jenny hurled the music box to the floor with all her might. There was a satisfying clang.

Norman stopped jumping and stared.

'Norman! Look what you've done – you naughty boy!'

At the sound of the ruckus Mama entered.

'What's going on in here?'

'Norman's jumping on my bed Mama and now look what he's done. He's broken Sofia's box.'

Norman shook his head, bewildered.

'Norman, get down from there, immediately!'

'No' me. No' me.'

Mama spanked the back of his podgy legs.

'Norman. How could you?'

'No' me. Mama!' Norman wailed, his face creased up with sudden tears.

Jenny almost felt sorry for him.

'Go to your room. Mama's very angry with you.' Mama sighed as he rushed from the bedroom and then her eyes narrowed and she turned. 'Jenny?'

Jenny squirmed, sensing her suspicion.

'Jenny, look at me.' Mama grabbed her chin.

'I have been as good as gold!' Jenny cried out.

Mama hesitated then drew her into a hug. 'It's all right Jenny, all right. It was an accident.'

But it was not all right.

Sofia had turned pale and had not spoken a word to anyone all day. Served her right, Jenny thought. But that evening Papa examined the broken box and Jenny was surprised to see the sadness in his eyes. He seemed close to tears. It was only a stupid music box, she felt like shouting.

'We will fix it Sofia,' he declared. 'I will fix it.'

And so now every evening, once the table had been cleared after supper, Papa would spread some old newspaper and spend hours trying to mend the box with Sofia shmia positioned opposite, eyeing his every move. They would murmur together in the funny lingo, which Mama said was called Yiddish, and sometimes they would even smile. With great care Papa repaired and glued the decorative edge which had splintered and broken. He came home with just the right colours of paint which he applied to the lid with a fine brush until the box itself looked almost as good as new.

Finally he opened up the compartment that contained the mechanism.

'Perhaps we should take it to Sol Levy?' Mama suggested.

Papa shook his head and looked across the table to Sofia and patted her hand. 'I will fix it.'

Jenny could contain herself no longer. She was helping Mama, drying the dishes after supper. 'It's just a stupid box!'

'Yes,' Mama replied. 'It is nothing special. A cheap trinket really.'

Jenny brightened. At least Mama could see how silly Papa was to make such a fuss, fuss, fuss.

'But for Sofia it is the most precious thing she has in the whole world. A gift from her parents.'

Jenny frowned. 'So why don't they mend it? And why doesn't she go home to them?'

Mama pulled the plug and the water drained from the sink.

'They have no home. And maybe her parents...' Mama put a hand on Jenny's shoulder. 'Well, but we won't think about that. For now we must look after Sofia. Mustn't we?'

Jenny rubbed the plate very hard. Inside she felt madder than ever and she wanted to shout. 'What about me!' But she knew it would be useless. Everything was useless. She sniffed and her lips trembled. Tears were welling up. She was going to cry.

Then there was a tinkling sound from the dining room and Mama was gone. Silence.

Jenny moved to the hallway and straining towards the open door, she heard the key being wound in the music box as far as it would go.

The tune began again. Mama exclaimed in delight.

Jenny ventured into the room. Norman was jiggling with excitement and Sofia was clapping her hands. And Papa, *her* Papa was grinning from ear to ear.

It was terrible.

But as the notes rose to a crescendo they faltered and stuck, repeating. Clang. Clang. All of them, Mama, Papa, Norman and Sofia froze and stared at the broken music box which would never be perfect again.

Clang. Clang.

Jenny looked at Papa, his fallen face, and then more than anything in the world she wished that the music would come back.

I Know How You Feel

PAUL ARNOLD

Ethel gripped the guard rail so hard that her hands hurt in an almost reassuring way. She examined her white knuckles then peered at her relatives on the quay who had come to see her off on her great – *once in a lifetime* – adventure to New York. It was her twenty-eighth birthday.

They seemed so small. She was already missing them and the journey ahead was long and worrying. She looked up at Queen Mary's three tall red and black funnels.

A horn blast reverberated over the dirty water. The huge ropes were retracted and the liner moved from the quay, tearing her from England. The water churned round the hull as it moved down the Mersey. Ethel's friends and family slowly shrank. It felt unreal. It had been so easy to accept the invitation, and now she had to do it. She was trapped.

George had sent her the ticket. He had visited them in England on his European tour. George was noisy, jolly, very bossy and American. He was a distant relative but he thought of himself as English. His wife had died in 1929, the year the world had become difficult. He had a firm handshake and insisted on buying everyone drinks.

She said she wanted a return ticket. She was in Cabin 327, first class, with a porthole. She closed the curtains hiding the grey clouds.

Ethel had once been to Ostend – the foreigners call it Osteende for some reason best known to themselves – for a day, but America was serious, yes; serious, serious.

The ship reached the open water and moved in a way that made Ethel feel queasy with the swell of the Irish Sea.

She unpacked one of her three new leather suitcases. The labels said CUNARD LINE. So *chic* – one of her new words for the trip. Threw her new clothes into the wardrobe. Ruffles and elegant lines. She had read that they were glamorous, movie-star-inspired. Feminine. Caped-back dress and fancy collar. Another dress in a nautical style.

She could not wait one minute longer. Ethel explored the ship.

There were two indoor swimming pools, beauty salons, libraries, and children's nurseries for each of the three classes – it wouldn't do for them to mix – a music studio and lecture hall, telephone to anywhere in the world, and dog kennels. This was the first ocean liner to be equipped with her own Jewish prayer room. To remind potential travellers that the smarter German liners didn't have one.

The largest room was the grand dining salon, spanning three storeys and supported by imposing columns. The balloon dances were simply divine. Partners had to support a balloon with their foreheads.

It was such fun. The men were good dancers and smelt quite delicious.

Every evening she dined with different people. They were all so interesting and amusing and witty, making her feel dull and plain.

They talked about American films they loved.

Gold Diggers of 1933. All the 'gold diggers', except Fay, end up married to wealthy men. The song, '*We're in the money*', that's where it's from. Ethel had seen it at the Majestic back home so didn't feel so out of touch.

On the fourth day the Statue of Liberty appeared, white in the mist.

The customs officers waved Ethel through. It was so exciting. George had come to meet her and hugged her for just a little too long. They walked to his grey Plymouth with white-walled tyres and he put her cases into what he called the trunk. As he drove, George proudly pointed out the landmarks of his city.

So that's what a skyscraper looks like. The Empire State building, so high. Ethel couldn't believe it. George promised they would go to the top tomorrow. There was so much to see. Perhaps a cruise round Manhattan Island? Broadway? Whatever Ethel wanted she could have.

His house was made of sandstone and faced a little park. A friendly black woman called Hattie opened the door and kissed her on the cheek. Ethel had only seen black people in the movies, but Hattie was very nice.

A band marched past the house. Red and black flags with a symbol she couldn't make out. George said, 'It's the German American Bund making that damned noise. Bastards. They should be shot.' He didn't say why.

The next morning she couldn't get out of bed. Her heart pounded and she couldn't breathe, and if she tried to stand up, her legs turned to jelly. She felt helpless and alone. Ethel was quite convinced that she was going to die and tears ran down her face. George called a doctor who examined her carefully.

'Can't find anything. Except a slight temperature,' he said. 'Have you been away from home before?' He smiled.

What a horrid rude man.

A few days after her partial recovery, George had too much to drink. He lunged at her so she ran round the table. George tripped on the carpet and she sprinted upstairs and locked the bedroom door. It was ridiculous, like something out of the movies. Now she understood his generosity: how could she have been so naive?

And then, next morning she planned her escape. She discreetly called a cab. Said she was going shopping. Hattie smiled, but thankfully, George was nowhere to be seen. Ethel phoned Cunard from a call box, the boat was only half full. 'It's the economy,' they said.

The liner moved sadly up the grey Mersey, dragged by three tugs.

Then the train home. Back to her little town – that until recently had been her entire universe. The houses seemed absurdly small. How could people drive along its narrow roads? Even the people felt smaller and slower.

*

Despite being back with her family, she missed New York. Its life, its noise, its big brashness. The colours — the foreign people, the smells. Its roaring energy. Had she imagined it all?

After six weeks she'd had enough. She had to go back. She paid for her ticket using her aunt's generous allowance. Second class, no porthole.

People were leaving Europe. Life was becoming more difficult.

She dined with a German doctor, his wife and two Canadians. The wife was so elegant and wore a pearl necklace.

The doctor had an awful lot to say in his nice English. He was going to a medical conference in Boston. A scientist had discovered the first effective antibacterial drug, something called Prontosil. His discovery had been published in Germany's top medical journal. German science. The best in the world.

'Herr Hitler has got Germany back to work. I don't agree with everything he's done but he has created full employment and built new roads. Ended strikes and crime. In many ways he is like Roosevelt, but more determined.' His voice became louder which wasn't really necessary. 'German jobs for all German workers, yes. All aliens must leave and many already have. A pure, prosperous Germany.'

The Canadian journalist said, 'Your leader has ordered twelve submarines in defiance of the Treaty of Versailles It really is very dangerous.'

They began to argue and started to speak in German, which was very annoying. Ethel thought it all sounded very exciting. Even better than the movies.

The next day happened to be Labor Day – whatever that was – and a storm blew up. There were only a few people in the swaying, clinking dining room. Staff scurried down the corridors carrying buckets and mops. A distinguished-looking man invited her to his table. He was a lawyer from Dresden who introduced himself as Edward Neumann. He spoke quite appalling English and was with his dishy son Reuben who smiled at her in an admiring sort of way.

The last two years had been terrible, Reuben said. He had been forced to leave medical school and his father couldn't have non-Jewish clients. They'd had to abandon everything in Berlin. He told her other unpleasant things. He was so sweet and it was sad but he did go on and on and the ocean was getting rougher. She was glad when she could go and lie down.

Ethel arrived in New York and rented a small apartment near Times Square. Her aunt's money would just about run to it. She bumped into Hattie in the cafe in Bloomingdales. Ethel had discovered bagels – quite delicious. Hattie already knew about them.

The next day Hattie brought George's nieces with her, introducing them as Miss Virginia and Miss Fanny. It was her day off.

Hattie said, 'He's got another one. I don't know how he does it. I know he's generous but he is a monster. You were lucky to escape. He broke his leg when he tripped on the rug. Thought you might like to know.'

Fanny said, 'No Southern woman is safe with that man.'

Virginia and Fanny were pretending to be Southern Belles today.

Fanny explained, 'We want to present a flirtatious yet chaste demeanour.'

Hattie said, 'What very silly girls you are.'

Virginia announced, 'We're going to acting school next semester. Georgy Porgy will pay, although he doesn't know it yet. He is made of money. We'll tell Mama we won scholarships.'

And for now they were going to spend the money for their piano lessons on betting and cigarettes. So there!

'We're going to the races at Belmont,' Virginia said. 'Next Wednesday. We'll go to Saratoga Springs on the train. Ethel can come too. Would you like that, Ethel?'

*

Ethel met them at Penn Station. It was seriously big, like the buildings she'd studied in history lessons.

Inside, the steel roof arches were like giant cobwebs across the huge spaces. Tubes of light beamed through the high round windows.

They bought tickets and the sisters giggled and sniggered at the other passengers. The train was packed with people going to the races. Beautifully dressed and talking too much. Perfumes and the aroma of gin floated down the carriages.

The sisters went straight to the racecourse's Champagne tent and Ethel followed in their wake. 'What pretty girls,' voices said.

They discussed the best way to bet. Ethel decided to stick with the favourites. Fanny would put her money on the smartest racing colours, Virginia on the best-looking ones. Fanny said, 'Do you mean the jockey or the horse?' and they giggled some more. The race started.

The jockeys in their colours crouched over the gleaming mounts, their sweating faces almost touching the horses' ears. The animals and tiny men thundered past the girls, throwing up clumps of soil and grass. The whips forced the mass of flickering muscle towards the finishing post. The blue and gold came first. Fanny's horse had won.

They slept on the train back to town. The sun, the excitement and the sisters' constant twittering had exhausted the three of them.

Ethel looked out across the flat farmland. She was getting bored with sightseeing and sitting in restaurants and, increasingly, in the bars that had opened everywhere. Fanny and Virginia only talked about themselves and fashion. She had heard all their stories. They were beginning to get on her nerves.

She met Hattie in Macy's. Hattie helped in a centre for homeless people run by her church.

Hattie said, 'I know they are all God's children but Jesus! – do they stink and some have gone a bit crazy. There are limits to what people can stand, I guess.'

Ethel remembered what George had said. 'Dammed hobos in Central Park, no other country would tolerate it. That bastard Hoover did it, now Teddy has to pick up the pieces, and we have to pay for it.'

Untidy huts were right in the middle of the park where the old lake had been. They looked like the ramshackle sheds people had on allotments at home to keep their spades and stuff. She could smell their wood fires and cooking and as she got closer the odours of unwashed people, poverty and crushed grass.

Tourists wandered round the chaos and misery sometimes handing out a few dimes, talking to the inhabitants and peering into their shacks.

Every day Ethel walked past the unwanted men on the street who tried to sell apples. Lost people from somewhere in Europe, grey, gaunt and hopeless, walked up and down Lexington Avenue.

It made her homesick again and she told Hattie.

Hattie said, '"By the rivers of Babylon, there we sat down, yea, we wept, when we remembered Zion."'

Ethel said, 'Yes, that kind of thing.'

'You should tell the homeless folks your story, they'd be real interested.'

Ethel wanted to look her very best. She chose a modest elegant black dress and had her hair done at Bloomingdales. She decided against the white gloves.

The hall was bare and cold. Her audience was huddled round a big wooden table.

Ethel stood in front of them, little butterflies fluttering inside her. She took a deep breath and told them her story. Of the pains of homesickness, how she thought she was going to die, of missing friends, of unfamiliar food, of the storm. Leaving Liverpool. Dreadful George and his appalling caddish behaviour. Of missing England and then America.

Ethel expected sympathy and perhaps just a little admiration. She hadn't realised how badly life had treated her before, but now, as she was telling her story, she became quite tearful.

A modest tale of heroism and fortitude. So far so good. They seemed interested as they devoured the free food.

She paused for breath and dramatic effect and a few smiled politely.

Then she rolled the well-intentioned sentence towards them. 'I know just how you poor people feel.' It took several seconds to explode.

Someone started to laugh. It was contagious. It got louder and harsher. A man started to cough and clutched his chest.

Perhaps it was time for another holiday.

Fruitellas

B E ANDRE

He's standing in the far corner of the tennis court, gripping the fence, when I finally spot him. Even the usual stragglers have gone in.

I swallow my strawberry-flavoured chew. 'Sayid?'

Nothing.

'Sayid,' I repeat, approaching him. Hoody and trainers, I notice – again. His blazer's probably scrunched in his bag. It's not the time to reproach him for his lack of regulation footwear.

'Go away, Miss. Please.'

I hear a clatter high up behind me and glance round.

'Miss Jenkins?' The deputy head calls from the first floor window of the science block. 'Is everything all right?'

I raise my hand in a gesture of *not now*.

He understands, nods, closes the window and leaves Sayid and me to fathom it out for ourselves.

I hold back a moment. 'I'm not going anywhere. Tell me what's the matter?'

No reaction.

'Are we going to stay here all day, Sayid?' I place my hand on his shoulder.

He jerks away. 'I can't stand it. I wish they piss off. All of them. Everyone at the home. And here.'

I don't mention his language but ask him what *they* did.

'They say it again, Miss.'

'What?'

He hesitates then kicks one foot with the other. 'Jihadi John. They don't stop, Miss.'

Jihadi John. I see. I can guess which of the little racist fuckers came up with that one.

What am I going to tell him? Look, Sayid, life is crap and that's the way it is. And by the time you're fifteen, there's going be a whole new pile of crap. Sixteen? Another pile. You might as well get used to it. It's your lot.

I ought to say we should go and fill out an incident form. Follow the correct procedure.

He hasn't even looked at me yet. I wonder if Sayid knows I love him, have loved him ever since he appeared in my tutor group two years ago. A dark-haired, skinny, tiny-scrap version of my nephew.

Loved him when I found him hiding in the cupboard after he was a no-show in the roll call for the fire drill.

Loved him when he'd suddenly slide off his chair and cower under his desk or crawl on his belly while I took the register.

Loved his excitement when I gave him an unused Man U stationery set found in the back of my son's wardrobe. I told Sayid I was born in Old Trafford and once went out with the captain of Manchester United. Slightly embellished, and good enough to make me a star in his eyes.

Loved his faith in me when the football breakthrough led him to confide he couldn't sleep at night in the children's home. He said his mother's headscarf, floating out to sea, filled his eyelids.

Risks. There would be no progress if not for risks. Now, it's my turn.

I could be disciplined for professional misconduct. Sayid could lash out at me and I'll have brought it on myself. Never touch a pupil. Never get too close to a pupil. Do not give false hope to damaged children. But if I don't do it now, perhaps I never will. He *needs* what I can give him.

'Sayid?'

'What, Miss?'

'Shall we have a hug?'

He turns round slowly, wiping the hoody sleeve across his face, 'Yeah, OK.'

He puts his head on my shoulder and his arms around my waist. Breathes in. 'Life's shit, innit, Miss?'

'Yeah,' I say.

'Yeah.' He sniffs up the glob of teary snot that's been threatening to slip down to his lips. 'Got Fruitella, Miss?'

Life Exchange

CLIFF CHEN

Ireland

But this rain, man. It come like nothing, soft-soft, invisible to man eye. You feel is damp breeze you walking through, until light catch it so: See it? *Mist*, brother! Watch it twirling under streetlights. This place not easy.

Trinidadians have the good sense to 'fraid rain. In our country it does pelt lightning behind you, and thunder to shake heavens. So first time we see Irish rain, we *stupes*: 'That little thing?' And we gone through it. Fake-out rain, I call it. Well brother, you reach home and you not *Trini to de bone* no more, all that done get wash out — is only chilly to de bone, right through. Ever see a Trini with the shivers? God never make a more wretched creature. Them rattling from the *inside*. When you watch them in their eye so, them serious-serious, like them just want to dead. See rain? Watch it good. You might as well be underwater. Trinis, walk with your goggles!

But them Irish don't study it. It come like is nothing.

The other day, they find one of us dead in a bedsit. Sitting up under the bedcovers, they find him – mister Bane – with his afro comb still sticking out. Eyes wide open and hands clasped in his lap, like he saying prayers, or trying to ride-out on an imaginary broomstick. Man freeze to death, just so. Funny how freeze to death could resemble electrocuted to death and scared to death, all rolled into one; death by suspicious circumstances. That's one thing sure.

I ended up knowing him, only because I was the second Trini to arrive in Galway. Bane, he was the first. And if you see cut-eye that man give me: morning, noon and night, like he want to fight. I think, 'What I do to this man?' My first Irish friend – he dead too, incidentally, from falling off the Salmon Weir bridge –

he had explain how things was before I reach. Bane was God.

Thing is, Irish people used to love a good foreigner. Somebody they could admire, and say to themselves, 'Why look at this exotic flower. Let's dig it up and walk around with it.' Get seen with Bane that time and you was a minor celebrity; your profile get raise one-time, for being in his crew. Who wouldn't want that? As for woman — don't talk, brother. That man was brushing everything in sight. One house party, I hear, the girls them form a line.

So now I reach. I not big like he, but I alright looking — have a little mix-race thing going. As for this pot of gold he find here, I had no clue about that. That's why my first friend wasn't nobody really. Just some fella who walk up to me in school and ask me if I does play chess. Well I tell him, yes; thinking about the oblong piece of cardboard me and my cousin spend whole morning colouring black squares on, because we didn't have a chess board, and then all kind of twigs, bottle-cap and old cork we dig up for pieces. In the end we couldn't find enough to match and had to make up a new game: checker-chess. It was alright. But that first

107

week in school, I didn't have no friends, so I say, 'Yes, in fact I do play a little chess.' And that seem to please him. Only later I start to realise, I could pick and choose my crew — just like Bane. By then me and Bane was mortal enemies, without exchanging one word.

Part of me knew that if I went up to Bane early on and try to make peace, even he would've been relieved not to be enemies anymore. But it still would've end in blows. Them Irish boys don't pass up chance to see a good fight. If they saw us talking, they would've close the circle one-time and shout fight, fight, fight — and start to pass money and odds. Them not easy.

My first Irish friend, he had done see that already. Looking back, is shame I feel now when I think about how they used to treat him. 'Nancy!' they shouting. The man trying his best to run some ball in P.E., up and down the gym — sticking his foot in, sliding tackles, all that — and they at the side shouting, 'We love you, Nancy! We love you! You-hoo!' I thought it was some boys who didn't realise Nancy was in my crew, cause them see me watching all this and start to carry-on even louder. Sad thing, really. Anyhow once I see that, I drop him one-time and start to think about crew. Nancy had his troubles, but I had Bane to think about. Wasn't long before those same fellas approach me, cool-cool they saunter up, already shape like a half-circle. They ask a few polite questions, crack a few jokes and as the conversation slide away from me, they start to spin stories. If you hear what them men was up to. I see a different side to Galway. Full of possibilities and excitement; not a checker-chess piece in sight. But the way those stories had come pouring out of them, fast-fast, I had wonder a little. One thing sure, they was nervous too. But I laugh anyway and whole time I laugh, I thinking: 'I reach now. Watch crew, right here.'

Nancy just went about his business, like he had expect it. He remain polite in the school corridor; but I could see that look in his eye, like some me-shaped possibility had slip away from him. And behind that, something even bigger left wanting. I remember the last thing he say to me – the very day before he climb up on that bridge and just topple-out over the rushing water – he watch me with the new crew, and he say, 'So the audition went well.' And he smile, but like it strain his face. I don't know why, but the shittiness of that old chess set came back to mind. I couldn't figure out who he meant had audition — me or them? That was his parting gift to me, a soft drizzle of wisdom. It had come like nothing; but over the years done soak me, through and through.

Poor Nancy, didn't leave with he goggles.

*

Trinidad

Here locals have the knack of seeing you, without seeing you. Their idle gaze carried off somewhere while they fan away the heat, leaving long stubborn pauses before replying. They may suck their teeth; *stupes*. Foreigners shouldn't mistake any of this for rudeness. Although to be fair, a case could be made.

My favourite thing to witness is a fellow foreigner trying to buy anything from a roadside vendor. When I see this unfolding, I find a cool spot out of sight – often concealed behind a tree – and peep out with a sadistic anthropologist's eye. Street vendors are *Level 1* social skills here in Trinidad. Fail this and you fail everything.

There he stands amidst a gaggle of Trinis: sweaty-pink under a large canvas hat, shoulder bag, eager black socks shooting out of his sandals (for God's sake). He furtles from his money pouch a few careful notes, timidly demonstrated to attract the vendor's attention. Trinis lean-in from every side, some even reach around him, calling orders from behind the vendor. 'Two with slight pepper, one without.' All assured of service. He might as well be invisible.

More Trinis arrive, bark orders, and receive grease-spotted paper bags, leaving him standing there utterly perplexed. No words to match his frustration: ignored, enfeebled, their shouts sting like school-yard taunts. Vainly, he looks around the street for anyone at all who can see his predicament. And me flattened to the tree, stifling giggles. I can't afford to be drawn into this, or I'd be forced to take the situation in hand and buy the damn thing for him. Here is the problem. Your average tourist labours under the notion that he has to win eye contact for his presence to count. Not true. The Trini approach is to behave like no one else is there: see, without seeing. But you can't be taught it. Knowing Trini isn't the same as being Trini. Being requires him to let go of all civility and take the plunge. But in this dreadful heat, his blood-pressure rising – can he do it?

He didn't. And I saw the death of something in our tourist's eyes as he sloped away, useless notes folded into his wallet. No recovering from that. His only consolation is that he doesn't live here. After a short holiday in this Caribbean paradise he will return home, where this anecdote will be spun for various friends. With each telling their awed reactions, their indignations, will rebuild him. Not all of us are so lucky.

Time gets awful slippery in Trinidad. Without the agreed upon seasons, you sometimes have to stop and ask yourself what month it is in the rest of the world. There is never snow or hail; ice is found only in drinks, or being chewed noisily in the mouth. And the torpid progress of the local business machine can have your will to live entirely bled from you.

I still don't have a telephone that works. The internet is something cosmic that occurs in random, shifting pockets in my home; I track it from room to room, waving my open laptop before me. A technician arrives and scratches his head. He checks all the points to make sure they are connected – I already did this – and later, I find him in the yard eating mangoes from my tree. 'On break,' he explains to me.

Welcome to Trinidad.

First published in Wasafiri, Spring 2014

Those Who Sell the Guns

RICKI THOMAS

Even the most basic home is a thing of beauty. There may be a picture of a child now grown, or a special door frame that cannot be repainted because of the pencil marks showing that extra inch or two. To an outsider it is just like any other house. To the family within it is home.

Before and since my birth, my father worked abroad and thus I lived in many homes in several countries in my formative years, but the one I shall tell you about was the last we shared, the last before he left my mother and me. A home we were forced from without a choice. The home that retained our furniture, our clothes, my toys, their possessions and the precious photos of me as a baby and us as a family. Their marriage was already broken, not that I knew it then, and now so were we.

Tehran, Iran, 1975. We had been living in the country for two years and I loved everything about it. I had found my best forever-friend and we were so naughty together. I wasn't to know that San and I would be sisters one day. My father and her mother, having an affair. I thank the heavens we were too young to realise how badly they were behaving.

Until the beginning of June, I was having the best year of my life.

I attended the British School and each morning a minibus picked me up from outside our home. I never understood how the moon shared the sky with the sun. It didn't make sense then and, after all this time, I still struggle to comprehend how it all works. Silly things, mental blocks. Every morning I would gaze through the bus window, chugging along without a seat belt as was the norm in those days. I contemplated eternity, space, how on the face of this planet I was an ant, a tiny speck of nothing. It was the same on the way home; the moon never seemed to leave the sky, day or night. I'm sure it must have at some stage.

The Queen Mother came to our school in April, immediately before life went crazy. She wore a fussy hat and smiled a lot, nodding to people, her gloved hand shaking theirs and another and another. Not mine. I didn't see what the excitement was about; an old lady in a crinkly dress. How was I to know about royalty, having barely set foot in Britain my whole life? I still have the photo though. She opened a new wing of the school, I think, but it meant nothing to me, bar missing a few lessons.

The adult me knows the shah had recently created the Rastakhiz Party to monopolise political activity, causing unrest, and the Islamic Revolution was threatening. The Queen Mother's visit was important for Britain's relations with Iran.

During the two years we lived there, we frequented a drinking hole for expats. I'm sure it can't have been every evening, but that's how it seemed to me, and the best part was it gave me a chance to spend time with San. Our parents bundled us into a playroom with the other children and pacified us with a choice of 7Up or Coca-Cola served in small, shapely bottles with a straw. We were to watch over San's younger brother.

But as I have mentioned before, San and I loved to misbehave. It didn't take too long for us to become bored with the room, smelly from unchanged nappies and sickly toddlers, and we'd wait for the adults at the bar to be drunken and laughing. We would then sneak out, dart under the nearest empty table and hide. A year older, I was ringleader, and once I was certain we hadn't been seen, my hand would creep to the tabletop and relieve it of whatever half-consumed drinks remained. We shared wine, or beer, or whatever it was that day. It could have been whisky; we weren't bothered. And we were never caught. Not once. I believe that says more about our parents than us.

It was on one of these occasions, creeping stealthily from the room, that I noticed my dad's hand on San's mother's bottom. I shielded my friend from the scene, protective already, but it confused me because it seemed my mother knew. She was right there and she was laughing with their friends. It felt wrong to me, but what was I to know? San's mother was heavy with a child. I didn't know where children came from then.

During our spell in Iran, we spent much of our time with San's family; shared meals at each other's houses, trips to the mountains, the club, toy camel racing and Yahtzee tournaments. It wasn't just the two families; a whole group of expats got together regularly to eat, drink and be merry, but my favourite times were when San was by my side.

Like Easter just gone. There were no Easter eggs in an Arab country, as you would expect, so our parents had blown chicken eggs and filled them with molten chocolate. Licking the treat was too normal for us; we took ours to the bathroom and melted the chocolate with our hands, smearing it over our faces, into our hair, on the basin, the walls. Why were we so destructive, they cried when they found us and our handiwork? What could possibly make us behave in such a way? Dad and San's father shouted, faces beetroot and almost exploding, but neither of us cried. The barriers that still remain were already forming.

So the night we stayed at San's house and watched her father threatening my parents and his pregnant wife with a gun, we shrugged and returned to bed. Instead of topping and tailing, I cradled her in my arms while she sang to herself and banged her head on the pillow, something she did nightly to help her sleep. Back then her habit would annoy me; now I yearn to relieve that desperate child of the torment that compelled her to behave in that way.

Soon after, we took a trip to the Alborz Mountains, our two families. It was a day out, a chance to spend time together and do something fun. Trips like this usually included a large group of people – squeezing into Land Rovers, tatty and green, weathered by the searing sun – and the outings would be a trek towards Damavand, the volcano that watches over Tehran, or further to the Caspian Sea. They would bring hampers of food, including chocolate bars dotted with white from melting and setting repeatedly. This time it was just us.

We parked in a village and our parents paid for enough mules to carry us on a trek up the insubstantial path zigzagging up the side of the mountain. The adults

119

took an animal each, San's mother cradling her new-born son in a sling. San shared a mule with her brother and I was alone. I have no recollection of the day, because the return journey eclipsed everything that had ever happened in my life before. I'm sure we would have spent the day in the clear, thin air, eating flatbreads and playing, scanning the beauty of the country below us. But that is my imagination.

The truth was, when sitting atop my mule and rounding a corner, I saw a sight I wish I could erase from my memory.

Blood. Knives. Rifles. Sabres and more blood. Sunlight glinting off swords like laser beams as they sliced through robes and Persian flesh, staining, reddening. More blood than I ever want to see again.

My parents, San's parents, shouted. Her father grabbed San's brother and I slid off my mule and onto hers, behind her, burying my head into her shoulder, terrified.

'Don't look, children!' shouted my mother.

'Close your eyes!' yelled my father.

'Oh my God!' said hers.

Below us bodies littered the ground. Men clutched wounds as they staggered, desperate to escape. Our trek guides acted to protect our lives, though terrified themselves. The villager leading our trek panicked, shouting commands in Farsi to the man behind, but the path was too narrow for the animals to turn. There was no choice for our group but to continue forward into the fight and beyond. I saw nothing more, my eyes squeezed tight, face buried into the girl I loved more than anything. I believed we were going to die and I wasn't ready for that.

I didn't go to school in Iran again.

The company my father worked for, which also employed San's father, started withdrawing British citizens from their projects, chartering aircraft to remove them and their families from the country with scant warning.

Our cat had produced five kittens only weeks before, little mites that scampered throughout our flat, up the curtains and carpeted walls, running across my bed and back.

I loved them.

Mum drowned them.

I saw her through the kitchen doorway, the first in her hands, tears streaming down her scarlet-speckled face as she lowered it into a glass bowl of water. I screamed and screamed – Just William's Violet – until my throat hurt and eyes ballooned, and San's father, who was there instead of my own, restrained me, hiding my murderous mother while I kicked and scratched at him.

To this day I have never forgiven her. I can't. She tells me they wouldn't have survived without us. I wanted them to have the chance to try.

The next day I was given a suitcase and bundled into a car, carrying only two of my toys – a plastic gun and a squeaky hand puppet – and a book about Paddington Bear. They took the toys at the airport, promising they would be returned when we landed, and my mother and I boarded a plane. Despite my grief, I was excited, yet had no idea what was happening.

The flight, a hotel, a blur of hushed conversations while I happily played in the imaginary world I had built around myself, and then I was taken to our new home. It was a dingy place with a roof that swathed the sides like a misshapen mushroom, tiny dark rooms and damp wallpaper. There was a room for me and a room for my mum, but my father wouldn't be joining us. I asked questions of a mother who was now lost in a bottle and she would slur at me to go away. And soon it dawned on me that losing all my toys, bar a gun and a puppet, was just the surface. I had lost my father too. We had lost our home, our friends, especially my best friend, and our life. There was no money to live on.

*

Forty years have passed and my history is water under a bridge, but during my lifetime I have seen time and again the power of one war after another, destroying people's lives, ripping them from their homes and communities, stealing their loved ones.

People with hearts and souls will continue to lose all they have and be shipped from one shore to another, simply seeking some peace in which to live a humble life, yet be scorned by everyone they meet. Swarms? Cockroaches?

I sit with my head in my hands and sigh.

Will no one ever learn that the only people to benefit from war are those who sell the guns?

Printed in Great Britain
by Amazon